the
ANIMAL UNDIE BALL

by
RUTH
PAUL

SCHOLASTIC
AUCKLAND SYDNEY NEW YORK LONDON TORONTO
MEXICO CITY NEW DELHI HONG KONG

To a secret glade, once a year,
animals came from far and near ...

lots of shapes and sorts and types,
dressed in spots and dressed in stripes.

Animals big, animals small,
animals short, animals tall,

fabulous fun was had by all
at the Animal Undie Ball.

Behold, a scene of such delight!
Animals dancing through the night!
Zebras, rhinos, frogs and pumas
sporting fancy pants and bloomers,

waltzing with the blue baboon
to Cockatoo's delightful tune.
And yet it ended all too soon,
one night beneath the autumn moon.

It happened thus: the yaks and ox
cavorted in their daks and jocks,
when from outside arose a din.
"**Stop!**" squealed Pig. "You can't come in!"

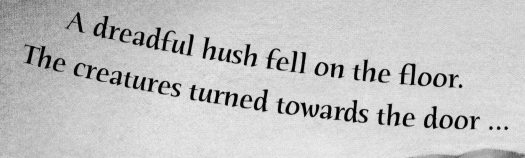

A dreadful hush fell on the floor.
The creatures turned towards the door ...

and there a fearsome sight they saw –
tooth and skin and scale and claw.

"HISSSSSSSSSSSSSSs," scowled Snake.

"Eeeerrrooooooo!" shrieked Elephant.

"Squaaaaaaaark!" cried Hen.

"Grrr," growled Spider ...

in their meanest, scariest voices.

Well ...

a frightened pack of fleeing foxes
got entangled in their boxers,
bowling down the blue baboons,
hiding in their pantaloons.

Out from under frilly scants
went Flamingo's spindly shanks,
squishing all the tiger-ants.
(What a bunch of scaredy-pants!)

Lion roared and clapped his paws,
hitching up his royal drawers.
"Settle down, now! Crikey dick!"
He looked ferocious. "Double quick!"

"Come on you lot –
spell it out!
What is all this
fuss about?"

Elephant sniffed
and drooped
his snout.

"The
problem
is ...
we feel
left
out."

"There are no undies in my size,"
he said with sad and downcast eyes.

"Perhaps you had forgotten this,
but Snake is leg-and-bottomless.

Whenever Hen wears underwear, her eggs all seem to disappear."

"Try to find an eight-legged pair," muttered Spider in despair.

"Gosh," growled Lion. "Fiddlesticks!
Underpants and politics?
Indeed I do not mean to mock –
but Snake, perhaps, could wear a sock?"

A titter spread across the hall.
Snake was not impressed at all.
"I suggessst," he hissed, "we all
wear sssomething elssse
to next year'sss Ball."

"I propose," said Hen, "a hat!"
Said Cockatoo, "I won't wear that."
"Then what about a scarf?" asked Dog.
"A vest would suit me more," said Frog.

And Lion, who himself liked boots,
announced, "I have the answer, troops.
Wild and tame, pets and brutes –
we all will wear our
Birthday Suits!

"Hooray! Hear, hear!" they all agreed -
for underpants they had no need.
(In fact, the only ones who do,
are creatures just like me and you.)

Animals big, animals small,
animals short, animals tall ...

nowadays they hold their Ball
with not a skerrick on at all!

For Chris, Eli and Billy

First published 2004 by Scholastic New Zealand Limited
Private Bag 94407, Greenmount, Auckland 1730, New Zealand

Scholastic Australia Pty Limited
PO Box 579, Gosford, NSW 2250, Australia

Scholastic Canada Ltd
604 King Street West, Toronto, Ontario M5V 1E1, Canada

Text and Illustrations © Ruth Paul, 2004

ISBN 978-1-86943-632-2

National Library of New Zealand Cataloguing-in-Publication Data

Paul, Ruth.
The animal undie ball / Ruth Paul.
ISBN 978-1-86943-632-2
[1. Underwear–Fiction. 2. Balls (Parties)–Fiction.
3. Animals–Fiction. 4. Stories in rhyme.]
I. Title. NZ823.2–dc 22

10 9 8 7 6 5 4   9/0   0 1 2 3 4 5/1

Publishing team: Christine Dale, Penny Scown and Annette Bisman

Typeset in 21pt Humana Serif